JUSTICE LEAGUE™

BLACK ADAM
AND THE
ETERNITY WAR

BY
DEREK FRIDOLFS

ILLUSTRATED BY
TIM LEVINS

STONE ARCH BOOKS
a capstone imprint

Published by Stone Arch Books in 2018
A Capstone Imprint
1710 Roe Crest Drive
North Mankato, Minnesota 56003
www.mycapstone.com

STAR39622

Cataloging-in-Publication Data is available
at the Library of Congress website.
ISBN: 978-1-4965-5981-4 (library binding)
ISBN: 978-1-4965-5988-3 (paperback)
ISBN: 978-1-4965-6000-1 (eBook PDF)

Summary: Black Adam banishes the Justice League — along with
Billy Batson and his heroic alter-ego Shazam — to ancient Egypt.
Can the heroes fight their way back from the past to defeat the
super-villain? Or will Black Adam conquer all of eternity?

Editor: Christopher Harbo
Designer: Bob Lentz

Printed in the United States of America.
010825S18

CONTENTS

When the champions of Earth came together to battle a threat too big for a single hero, they realized the value of strength in numbers. Together they formed an unstoppable team, dedicated to defending the planet from the forces of evil. They are the . . .

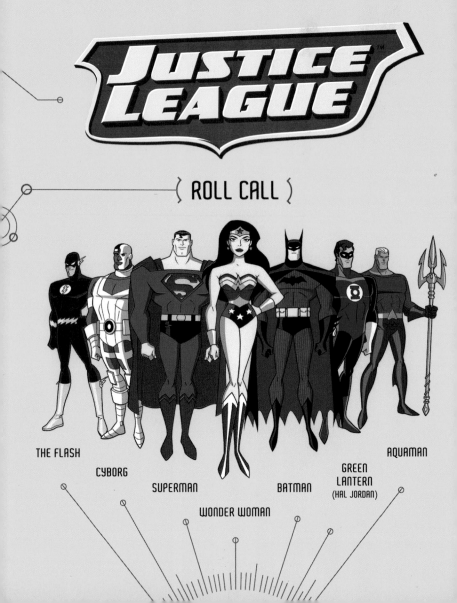

JUSTICE LEAGUE™

⟨ ROLL CALL ⟩

THE FLASH

CYBORG

SUPERMAN

WONDER WOMAN

BATMAN

GREEN
LANTERN
(HAL JORDAN)

AQUAMAN

MARTIAN
MANHUNTER

HAWKGIRL

HAWKMAN

GREEN ARROW

BLACK CANARY

GREEN LANTERN
(JOHN STEWART)

THE ATOM

SUPERGIRL

RED TORNADO

POWER GIRL

SHAZAM

PLASTIC MAN

BOOSTER GOLD

BLUE BEETLE

ZATANNA

VIXEN

METAMORPHO

ETRIGAN
THE DEMON

FIRESTORM

HUNTRESS

CHAPTER 1

DEAD RISING

Spectacular beams of sunlight glinted off the giant panels of a huge glass pyramid in downtown Metropolis. The city of tomorrow was host to many familiar landmarks, such as the Daily Planet Building and LexCorp Tower. But it was this triangular construction that captured the city's full attention today.

A large crowd gathered near the roped-off entrance, barely able to contain its excitement. Behind it a fleet of vehicles clogged the streets. The media had arrived to cover the event. Among them were two reporters who pushed their way forward.

"Um, excuse me. Pardon me," said Clark Kent politely. Two tall people in hats blocked his view. They ignored his request.

"Hurry up, Smallville! Or you'll be watching this from the bleachers," warned Lois Lane. She elbowed her way forward to find an open spot near the front of the crowd.

At a podium in front of the pyramid, the mayor prepared to address the crowd. Beside him stood a woman wearing glasses, a blue dress suit, and her dark hair pulled back. And on his other side stood Lex Luthor. The notorious businessman and criminal mastermind tugged at the lapels on his suit.

"Welcome on behalf of Metropolis and the United Nations, who sent their ambassador, Diana Prince," said the mayor, gesturing to the woman beside him. "We thank you for attending this opening ceremony."

The mayor continued, "This wonderful, state-of-the-art, cold fusion energy plant —"

"All thanks to the generous funding of LexCorp," interrupted Lex, stepping in front of the mayor with a smug smile.

"Yes, well, of course —" the mayor uncomfortably agreed, taking back his place at the podium. "We hope this facility will provide clean and safe energy. Not just for Metropolis, but for the entire region."

As the crowd applauded, Lois shook her head. "No one steals the spotlight better than Luthor, right, Clark? *Clark?*"

Clark lowered his glasses and squinted over them. Something was unsettling the crowd. It pushed through the people, making a sound that sent a chill up his spine.

GRUUUUHHH!

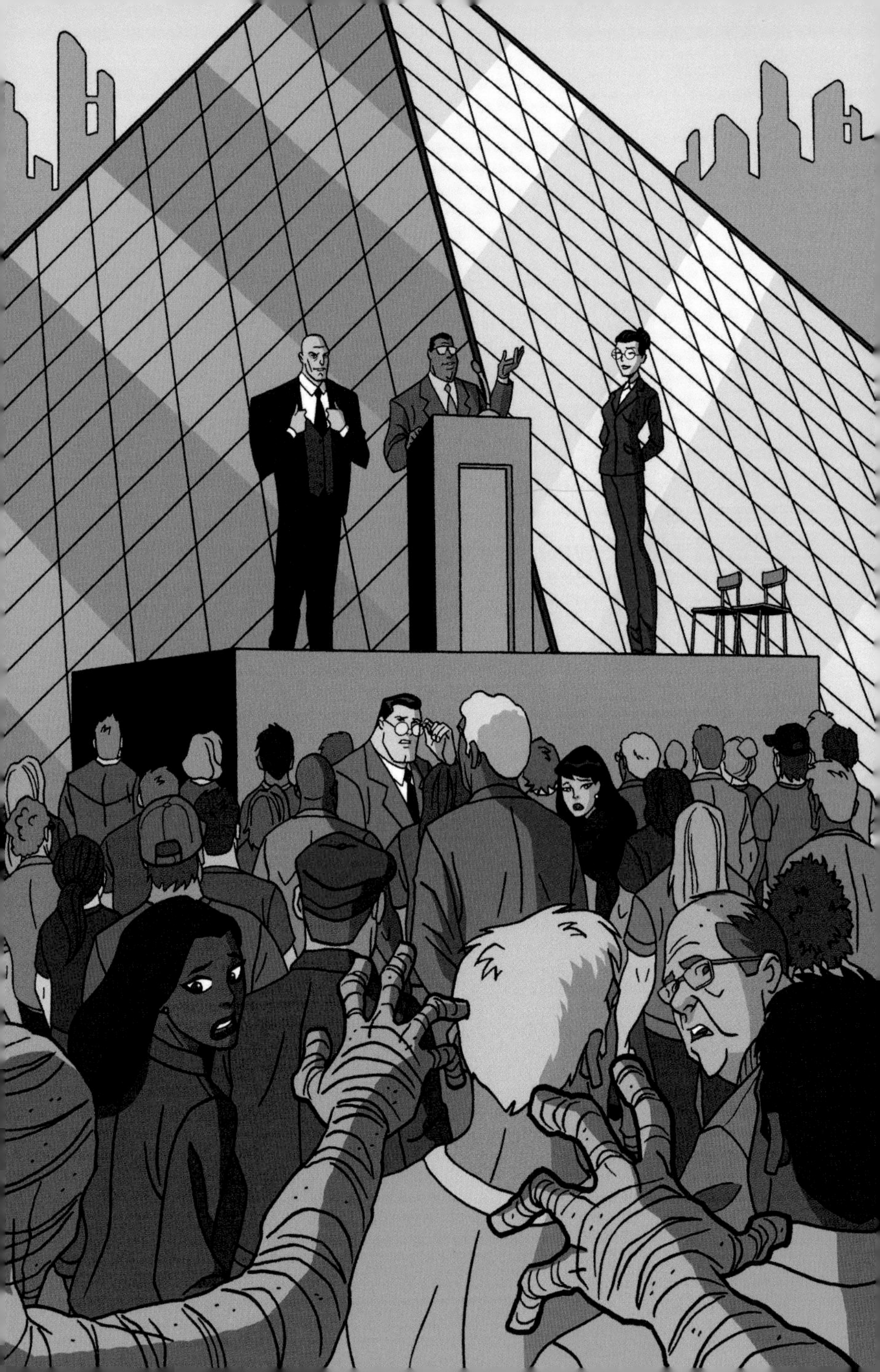

As the crowd separated in all directions, the cause of the commotion became clear. A horde of horrific mummies shambled forward! Wrapped in torn, dirty bandages, their feet scraped and dragged along the pavement. Their withered, outstretched arms reached for anything that moved.

"I think we have a new front-page headline," said Lois as a mummy tugged on her lavender jacket. She kicked the undead monster back with her high-heeled shoe.

"Head for the van, Lois!" shouted Clark. "I'll be right behind you."

As Lois ran through the panicked crowd, Clark dashed across the street and into a department store. Ducking into a dressing room, he removed his glasses, loosened his tie, and opened his dress shirt. Superman had arrived!

Meanwhile, Diana Prince ran into the glass pyramid and knocked on a storage room door. Hearing no reply, she slipped inside. In the blink of an eye, she emerged as Wonder Woman!

Outside, a mummy toppled the mayor's podium. It clawed its way toward him with its mouth stretched open.

"Help me!" screamed the mayor.

Before the mummy could bite, a golden lasso shot from the pyramid's entryway and wrapped around the bandaged body. Wonder Woman yanked the creature off the mayor and swung it into a tree across the street. The mummy shattered into a pile of dust.

Superman's red cape billowed behind him as he landed in front of the entrance to the pyramid. He used his super-breath to blow a group of mummies away from the crowd.

"Lex!" said the Man of Steel, turning to the bald man cowering behind his cape.

"I know what you're thinking. But I had nothing to do with this," said Lex. "Honest!"

Before he could offer any proof, two mummies grabbed Lex's legs and dragged him to the ground. While Superman punched the mummies, reducing them to dust, Lex scurried to his waiting helicopter.

"Mercy! Get me out of here . . . *NOW!*" Lex commanded his pilot.

Lex buckled into his seat as the helicopter lifted off the ground. A few mummies hanging from the copter's tail tumbled off.

As the crowd scattered in all directions, dozens of ancient mummies spilled forth. They rushed toward the entryway to the glass pyramid, determined to get inside.

Superman and Wonder Woman retreated inside to fend them off, but they were clearly outnumbered. For every five mummies they destroyed, ten more took their place.

"There are too many of them!" shouted Superman. He used his heat vision to burn a trench into the floor. He hoped it would stop the mummies from advancing any further.

"We must keep them from reaching the fusion energy core," warned Wonder Woman. "Even a small crack could cause a nuclear meltdown that would destroy all of Metropolis."

A sudden gust of wind bumped her tiara and blew her hair across her face.

"It's a good thing we're here then. Because I kinda like this city," said The Flash with a smile. "Be right back!"

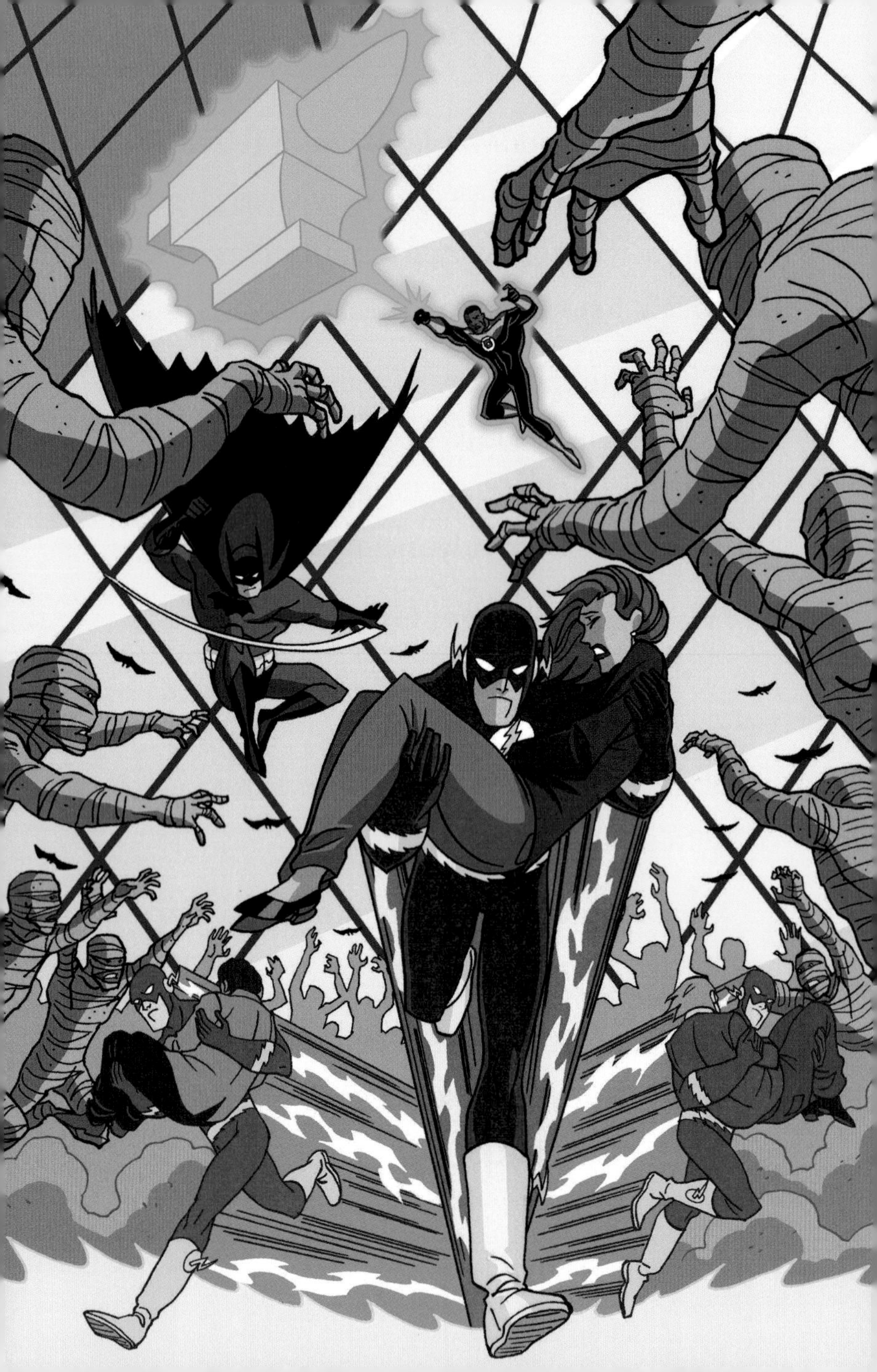

The Flash ran through the crowd of mummies. As the speedy red blur rescued innocent people, more members of the Justice League arrived. Batman glided to the ground, releasing a flurry of Batarangs. The well-aimed weapons turned half a dozen mummies into clouds of dust.

Coming up behind the Dark Knight, Green Lantern hovered in the air above the last remaining mummies. He used his power ring to create an oversized, glowing green anvil. Then he dropped it, crushing the creatures flat.

POOOF!!!

"I always wanted to do that," said Green Lantern.

"Well, that takes care of that," said The Flash. "Nice work!"

"This wasn't the only attack," said Batman as he walked over to Superman. "There have been more."

"Then we need to get back to the Watchtower," replied the Man of Steel.

"That's my cue," said Green Lantern. He used his power ring to create a giant bubble around the team. Then he carried them to the Watchtower, the Justice League's satellite headquarters in space.

Once inside they met a green-skinned alien in the command center. Martian Manhunter stared at his computer screens.

"How bad is it?" asked Superman.

"Every country on the planet has seen outbreaks of these armies of the undead," said Manhunter. "I've sent every available member of the Justice League to help."

Batman leaned closer to the computer screens. He could see mummies at various world landmarks. Their arms were raised, and they were chanting something.

"Turn up the volume," said the Dark Knight. "I want to hear what they're saying."

TETHHHH-ADAM!

TETHHHH-ADAM!

TETHHHH-ADAM!

Batman squinted. "It's an Egyptian name. But not one I recognize."

"I might know someone who does," said Superman. "But we'll need to find him in Fawcett City."

CHAPTER 2

SCHOOL'S OUT

WHACK!

A loose shoe flipped up in the air
as a soccer ball bounced across a dusty
schoolyard. Screaming in delight, a group
of children ran past young Billy Batson to
chase the ball down.

Ten-year-old Billy carried his backpack
as he walked across the playground with a
carefree smile on his face. Then he noticed
a group of classmates gathered around a
game. He changed directions to join them
when a blonde girl with pigtails burst from
the group crying.

"Thanks for your lunch, Sally," called Devin. "None of you can beat me. But go on and try. Who's next?"

Billy's classmates parted to reveal a tall boy with orange, spiked hair, a gap-toothed smile, and thick, muscular arms. Devin Chandler was two grades behind Billy — but he was always looking to pick a fight.

"Is that you, Billy Batty?" asked Devin.

"It's Batson," Billy corrected him.

"Whatever," shrugged Devin. "You gonna play me?"

"Not today," squeaked Billy, trying hard not to swallow nervously.

"Nah, it's definitely your turn. Don't make me come grab you," threatened Devin. "The game is Devin's Doom. The entrance fee is your lunch. Now pony up!"

Devin ripped Billy's backpack off, spinning him around. Tearing at the zipper, he shook the bag upside down. Some books, pencils, and an apple fell from it.

"That's it?! You're not even worth it," scoffed Devin.

Billy felt relieved to avoid the game. He started to grab his backpack, but Devin's meaty fingers squeezed his shoulder. "That's okay. Looks like you'll just owe me lunch for the rest of the week."

Devin grabbed a stick and drew a large circle in the dirt. "You know the rules," he said, picking up a small playground ball. "We stand in this circle and take turns chucking a ball. If you dodge or catch the ball, you keep playing. If you get hit or fall out of the circle, you lose. You go first!"

THWACK!

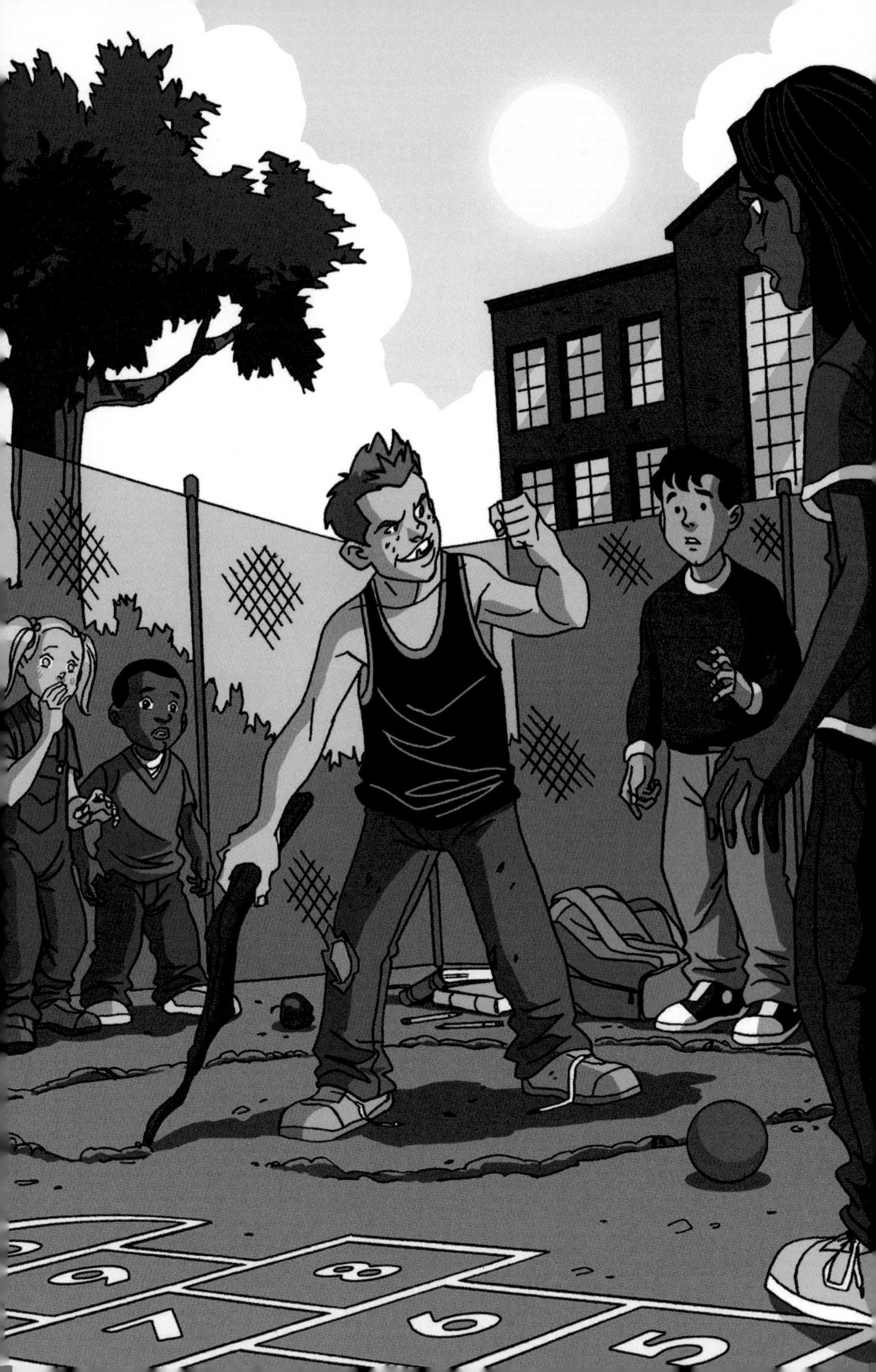

Devin threw the ball at Billy's forehead, knocking him to the ground. As the bully laughed, Billy got back to his feet and picked up the ball.

Standing inside the circle, Devin waved him on. "Come on. Just try to hit me. I know you can't!"

Gritting his teeth, Billy threw the ball with all of his might. The ball sailed through the air . . . and into Devin's waiting hands.

"Nice try, little loser. Now it's my turn," spat Devin.

THUDD!

Devin's ball hit Billy square in the stomach, knocking the air out of him. He hit the ground hard and slid out of the circle.

"Next time, why don't you try dodging? It's what you're good at," mocked Devin.

Devin walked away with the rest of the children. Billy began gathering up his belongings when a shadow fell over him.

"Aw . . . can't you just leave me alone, Devin? You got what you wanted," said Billy, expecting the bully to laugh at him. Instead, all Billy heard was creepy, labored breathing.

GRUUUUHHH!

Billy looked up. Standing over him was a huge, angry mummy with tattered bandages. It grabbed Billy by his shirt.

"Holy smokes! Get off me!" shouted Billy.

Squirming free, Billy fell backward. The mummy slowly lumbered after him until it heard a scream. Then it stopped, turned its head, and saw Sally over by the sandbox. With a new target, the mummy changed direction. It dragged its feet toward her.

Billy picked up the ball from the game and threw it at the mummy. It bounced harmlessly off its shoulder and landed back in Billy's hands. The mummy continued to stagger closer to the little girl.

"Run, Sally!" yelled Billy, shoving the ball into his backpack. But Sally froze in fear.

Billy knew what he had to do. To most people he was just a kid. But to those in need he was the World's Mightiest Mortal — Shazam!

Billy dropped his backpack, clenched his fists, and shouted the magic word that would transform him: "*SHAZAM!*"

Nothing happened.

"SHAZAM! SHAZAM! SHAZAM!" he said again and again. But he remained Billy Batson, fourth grade student.

"Why isn't it working?" Billy asked, looking at his hands in shock.

EEEEEEEEK! Sally screamed again as the mummy climbed into the sandbox. When its feet shifted in the sand, the mummy wobbled and fell to its knees. But it still crawled after the little girl. As it stretched out its arm to grab her, its own wrist was grabbed by something much stronger.

"Leave her alone!" commanded Wonder Woman, lifting the mummy over her head.

"I'd listen to her," said The Flash. He stood alongside the other members of the Justice League on the playground.

Using her Amazonian strength, Wonder Woman threw the mummy into the metal monkey bars. The mummy instantly crumbled to dust on impact. Then Wonder Woman bent down to give Sally a hug.

"Gosh! You're the Justice League," said Billy, running up to join the rest of team. "Thanks for saving us!"

Sally ran away and disappeared into the school. With the playground empty, Superman stepped up to Billy.

"We need your help, Billy," said the Man of Steel. "Will you join us?"

"I don't know how much help I'll be," said Billy. "I can't change into Shazam."

"Do you think it has something to do with these mummies?" Superman asked, placing a reassuring hand on Billy's shoulder.

"I don't know. But I know who might," said Billy with renewed excitement. "Come on! The Wizard will know what to do."

"Did he just say a wizard?" asked The Flash.

* * *

A short time later, Billy and the Justice League arrived in downtown Fawcett City. They trotted down a staircase to a subway platform beneath the bustling streets. When the last remaining adults on their way to work boarded the subway car, the heroes found themselves alone on the platform. Billy hopped down between the tracks and walked into the dark subway tunnel.

"It's okay," said Billy. "Just follow me."

The Justice League followed Billy a few hundred feet until a glowing reddish light appeared ahead of them. Parked on the tracks sat an impressive, red rocket train with sleek, gold trimmings. As if waiting only for them, its doors opened when Billy approached.

"This will take us to the Wizard. We don't even need a ticket," Billy said with a wink.

As soon as they stepped inside, the doors shut behind them. Then the train raced through the tunnel with blinding speed.

SCREEEEEECH!

They had only traveled what seemed like minutes when the train's metal wheels sparked. When it came to a gentle stop, the doors opened with a soft **HISSSS**.

"We're here!" exclaimed Billy, hopping down onto the stone floor.

"And where's here, kid?" asked Green Lantern. He used his power ring as a flashlight to cut through the darkness.

"This is the Rock of Eternity," announced Billy. "The Wizard who gave me my powers lives here."

Walking through the cave, they passed seven giant statues posing along one wall. Their human forms had oversized heads and looks of anger, sadness, envy, and other pained emotions. Written beneath them were the words THE SEVEN DEADLY ENEMIES OF MAN. Batman studied the statues with steel-eyed suspicion.

"Oh, don't mind them," said Billy. "The Wizard is up ahead."

The end of the cave opened up to reveal a large room with a few stone steps. At the top of the steps stood an empty stone throne.

"Where is the Wizard, Billy?" asked Superman.

"I just need to light the torch to make him appear," said Billy, pointing at an unlit torch mounted next to the throne.

Batman removed a small flare from his Utility Belt. He snapped off the top to ignite it before handing it to Billy.

Billy approached the torch and carefully lit it. A rising flame cast the room in a soft glow as smoke swirled around the stone throne. Billy and the Justice League awaited the arrival of the Wizard. What appeared in his place was someone else entirely.

A man dressed in black and gold now clutched the throne's armrests. The yellow lightning bolt on his chest looked similar to Shazam's. But his jet-black hair, sharp eyebrows, and pointed ears gave him a dark, villainous look.

"You called for me?" asked the man with a wicked smile.

"Black Adam!" Billy gasped.

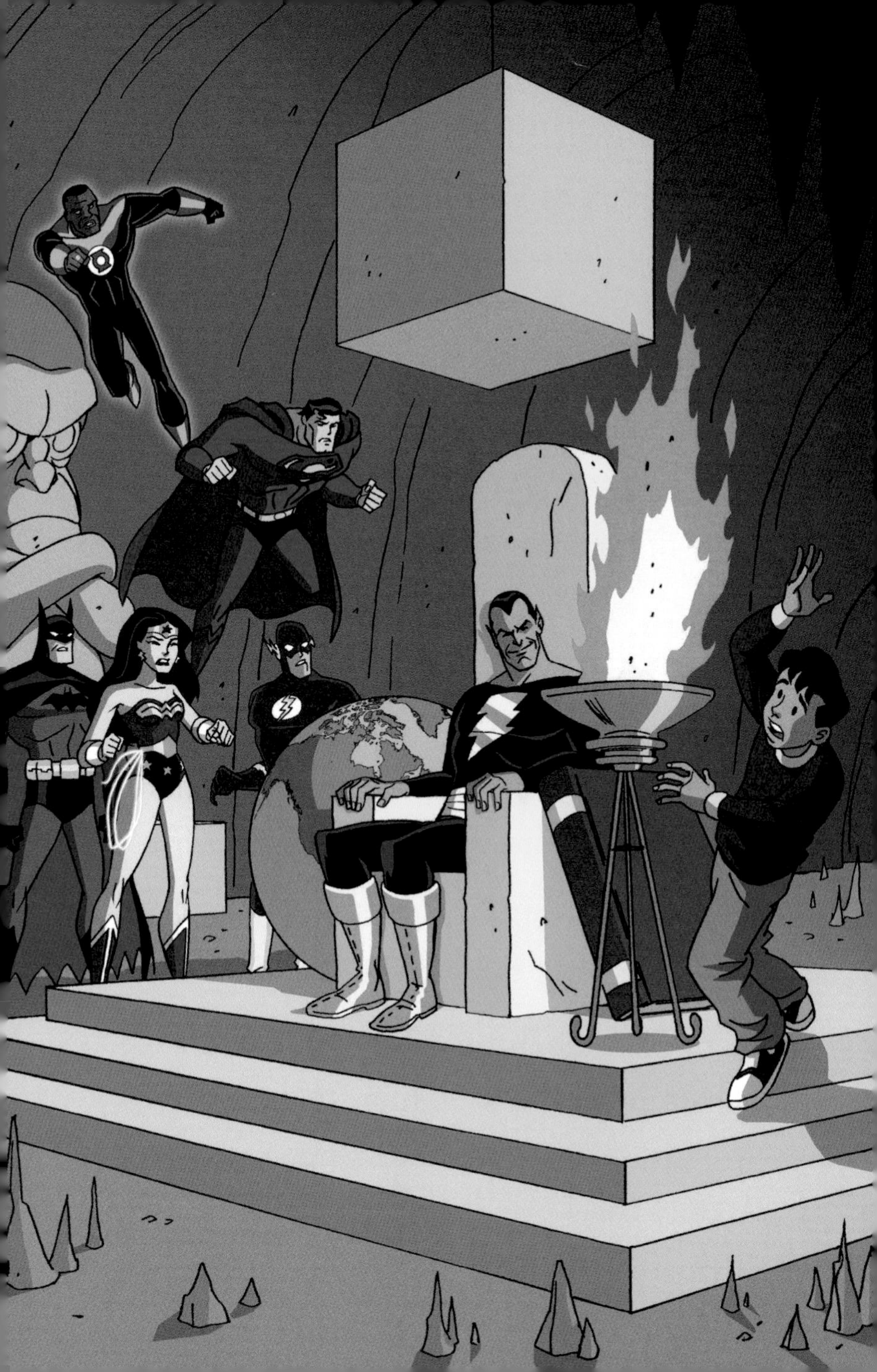

CHAPTER 3
WIZARD'S QUEST

"You don't belong here!" shouted Billy, pointing at Shazam's greatest enemy.

Black Adam leaned back in the Wizard's throne and laughed. "You are in my home now, brat! Bow before me." Clapping his hands, Adam sent a sonic shock wave that knocked everyone off their feet.

"You picked the wrong day to pretend to be the Wizard," said Superman.

Black Adam rose from his throne as Superman flew toward him. The Man of Steel swung a wide punch, connecting with Black Adam's cheek.

Superman's blow didn't even faze the villain. Adam returned a strong backhand. It spun Superman end over end, knocking him out as he crashed to the floor.

"The only imposters I see are you so-called heroes," said Black Adam.

"Spread out and hit him with everything you've got!" Batman yelled to his teammates.

Black Adam calmly walked toward them. Batman tossed smoke bombs onto the floor to provide cover. But Adam whooshed away the mist with a sweep of his hand.

As the smoke cleared, a golden lasso wrapped tightly around Black Adam's arm. The villain felt a tug on the rope, then he snapped his arm back to pull Wonder Woman off her feet. Twirling the Amazon in a circle, he flung her headlong into Batman. Both heroes tumbled across the cave.

Green Lantern used his power ring to construct an oversized magician's trunk. He floated it across the throne room and snapped it shut around Black Adam.

"Got him!" cheered Green Lantern.

But behind him Adam pried the trunk open. When Green Lantern turned back around, he stood face to face with the villain. Before he could create another construct, Adam grasped Green Lantern's ringed fist. He forced the hero down to one knee.

"My magic is better than yours," sneered Black Adam.

Pulling the hero to his feet, Adam forced Green Lantern to point his ring back at himself. Without warning, it began to glow.

"That's impossible!" Green Lantern exclaimed. "Only I can control —"

A blast of light launched Green Lantern into the ceiling. Then he collapsed to the floor with the clatter of broken stalactites.

The Flash was the only hero still standing. He ran toward Black Adam, zigzagging so fast he created a trail of blurred duplicates.

Black Adam simply snapped his fingers. Like a television remote, The Flash *PAUSED* in mid-stride. When Black Adam snapped again, all of the hero's blurred duplicates collided with The Flash, knocking him out.

With a twirl of his hand, Black Adam's magic lifted the Justice League into the air. They hovered above him as the villain sat back down on the throne.

"How do you like my trophies?" asked Black Adam, grinning at Billy. The boy could only clench his fists, staring helplessly up at his friends.

"Oh, do you wish to save them?" asked Black Adam. "You're free to try."

Without the power of Shazam, Billy was just an ordinary kid. What could he do to stop someone so powerful? Even with these doubts, Billy knew he had to try something. He couldn't just stand by and watch Black Adam win if it meant others would be hurt.

Billy set down his backpack. Then he closed his eyes, took a deep breath, and charged his enemy —

After only a couple steps, Billy tripped on a small rock sticking up from the floor. *THUDD!* He fell flat on his face.

HA! HA! HA! HA! HA! Black Adam laughed so loud it echoed throughout the cavern. He stared up at the Justice League. "If this is your champion, then your planet is truly doomed."

"Teth-Adam," said Batman, still hovering in the air. "The name the mummies chanted. They were calling to you."

"Correct," replied Black Adam. "It's a name I haven't heard for centuries. But it's a name my followers knew very well."

"The mummies are your followers brought back from the dead," concluded Batman.

"What did you do to the Wizard?" asked Billy, shaking his fist at the villain.

"I defeated him," said Black Adam with a sneer. "And it was easy. The last time we fought, you were Shazam. After our battle I followed you to this tunnel and found the Rock of Eternity. Once you left, I alone faced the Wizard and stopped his reign of terror."

"The Wizard is good. He gave both of us our powers," said Billy.

"And he wasted their use, much like you," replied Black Adam. "What good is all the power in the world if it's not used for the right purpose?"

"But you used it selfishly for evil," explained Billy. "That's why the Wizard took your power away and gave it to me."

"But not anymore," countered Black Adam. "After defeating the Wizard, I gained all of his power and removed all of yours. Then I used the Rock of Eternity to send the Wizard away. Not across space like he did to me, but through time. And now all of you will join him!"

With a wave of his hand, Black Adam opened a time portal. The dark void sucked the Justice League and Billy inside. In an instant they were gone.

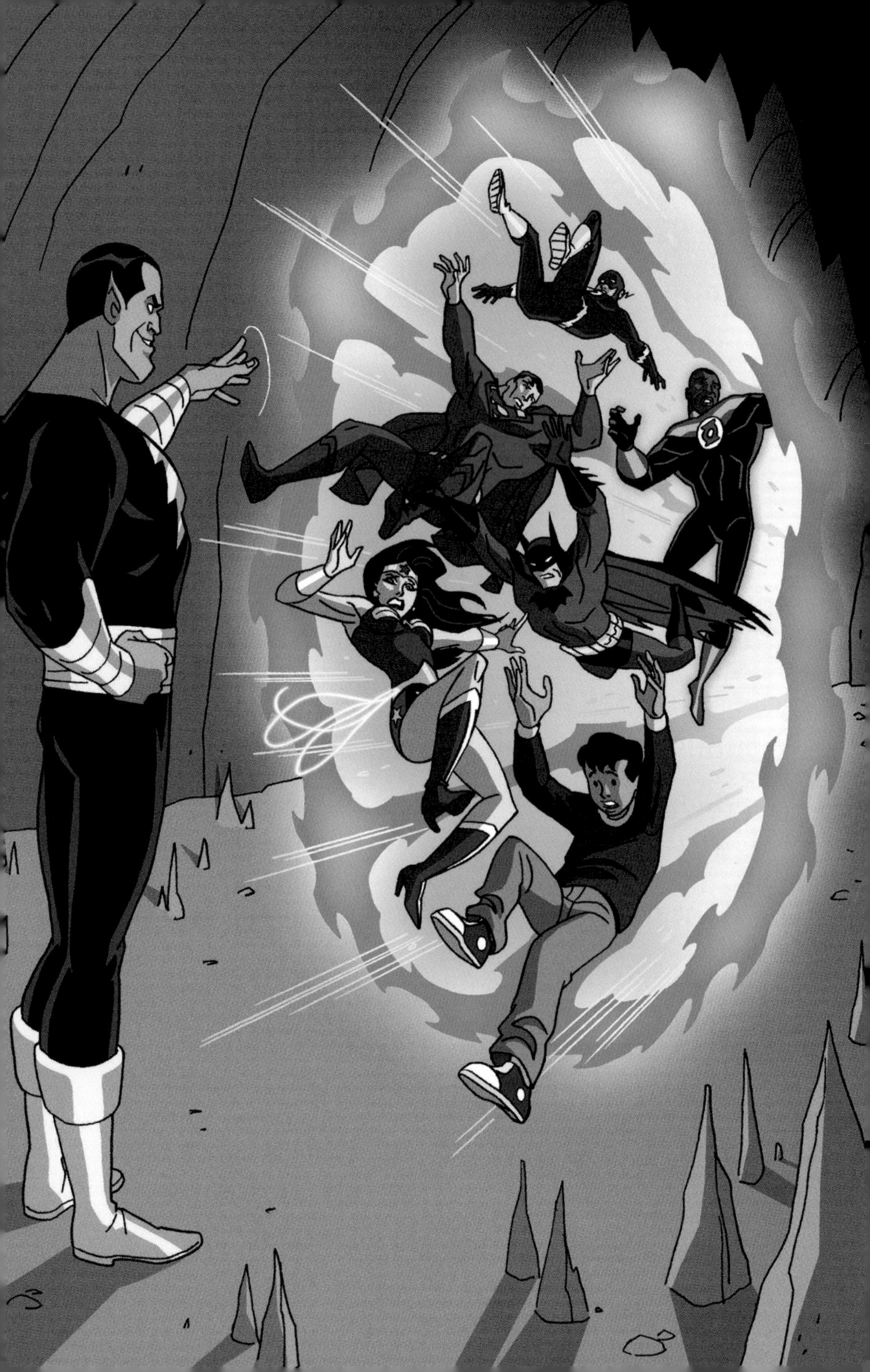

* * *

SKREE·BOOM! A loud impact in the desert released a giant dust cloud. Billy woke up in the center of a huge crater. He blinked rapidly to remove sand from his eyes. Then he sat up enough to see the Justice League waking up beside him.

The team climbed out of the crater to find themselves surrounded by sand dunes. In the distance Billy spotted a Sphinx statue outlined by the setting sun. The sight of it made him feel ill. Billy knew they were far from home, both in miles and years. Black Adam had sent them back to ancient Egypt!

Green Lantern squinted at the statue and the city that lay behind it. "We've got to get into that city."

"And find the Wizard," added Billy.

"I suggest we wait for the cover of darkness," said Wonder Woman.

"Good plan for you guys," replied The Flash. "But how about I do my zoom zoom thing while you wait? I'm sure I can track down the Wizard with Billy's help."

"I say we give them a shot," Superman said to Batman. "We can meet back up at the base of the Sphinx after nightfall."

Batman nodded and turned to The Flash. "Look for the pharaoh's palace. It's your best bet for finding the Wizard."

"You got it," said The Flash. "Climb aboard, Billy. And hold on tight!"

The Flash raced off through the city's streets, leaving only a swift night breeze in his wake. Soon after nightfall they stopped for cover near an empty, outdoor market.

"That must be the palace over there!" Billy said, pointing down a side street.

At the end of the street stood a grand fortress made up of columns, arches, and statues. A tall, heavily guarded stone wall surrounded the entire building.

"How will we get inside unnoticed?" asked Billy, spotting the guards around the wall.

"Leave that to me. You just keep an eye out for your friend," said The Flash.

Timing it just right, The Flash raced around and between the guards patrolling the palace. Only one noticed the sudden, pleasant breeze blowing past him.

Then The Flash carried Billy through the palace's many corridors and rooms. Unable to find the Wizard, they stopped near the pharaoh's chambers when they heard voices.

"What news do you bring?" asked the pharaoh. He paced back and forth across the chamber as he took off his royal headdress.

"The foolish old man still thinks he is some kind of god," reported the pharaoh's personal guard.

"Very well. I will deal with him in the morning," said the pharaoh, waving his guard away.

"As you wish," agreed the pharaoh's guard, exiting the chamber.

As the guard walked down a stone staircase, The Flash and Billy quietly followed. At the end of the dark hall, the guard kicked a locked cell door as he passed.

"Enjoy your last night, old man," the guard whispered before rounding the corner and disappearing.

The Flash tiptoed up to the cell door, and Billy climbed off his back. Then The Flash vibrated his hand to chop at the lock. When it broke, Billy caught it before it crashed to the floor.

As the door quietly creaked open, Billy and The Flash peeked into the darkness. An old man wearing a robe was sitting on the ground. He had a bald head and a long, white beard.

"Wizard? Is that you?" asked Billy, stepping forward. "It's me . . . Billy. Billy Batson."

"Billy?" said a frail voice. "He sent you here too? I am so very sorry."

Suddenly, shadows appeared on the wall behind them. They were followed by the sound of guards approaching the far end of the hall.

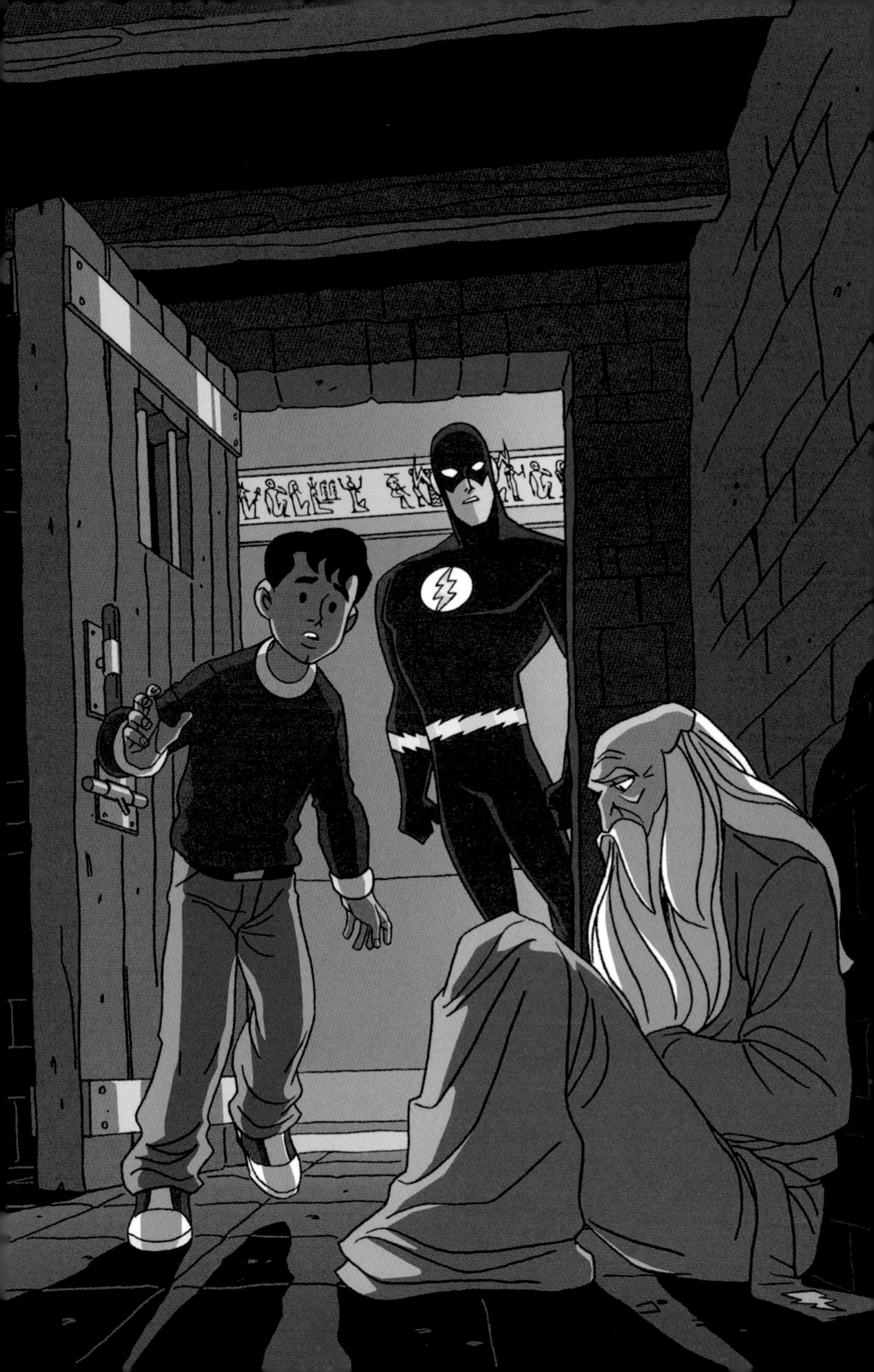

"We can talk outside. But we have to go now!" said The Flash, scooping the Wizard up in his arms.

Billy hopped onto The Flash's back. As they ran past the advancing guards, The Flash's speed snuffed out their torches. Once outside the palace, The Flash and his companions rejoined the rest of the Justice League at the base of the Sphinx.

"Okay . . . do your thing," said The Flash, helping the Wizard to his feet. "Alakazam and all that!"

"I can't," said the Wizard, hanging his head in shame. "Black Adam took my powers just like he took Billy's. I'm afraid we're all stuck here."

"You mean we can never return home?" asked Superman.

"I just don't believe it," said Billy. "There's got to be some way back. Something you haven't thought of."

The Wizard looked out at the pyramids in the distance, and his eyes opened wide. His long white beard couldn't hide a smile spreading across his face. He placed a hand on Billy's head, ruffling the boy's hair.

"You're right, Billy. There is one chance," said the Wizard. "Follow me."

CHAPTER 4

THE TRIALS OF SHAZAM

Using the cover of darkness, the Justice League followed the Wizard to a pyramid rising out of the desert. Its entrance was sealed tight, but it was no match for Green Lantern's power ring. He created a giant pickaxe that pried out a stone large enough for them to enter. Inside the air was dry and cold. Batman handed out flares from his Utility Belt to use as torches.

"In this time grave robbing is punishable by death," said the Dark Knight.

"Then it's a good thing we're only stealing a chance to return home," said the Wizard.

The Wizard held his torch up to the wall. A series of hieroglyphs covered the stone surface. The Wizard studied the symbols closely, stroking his beard.

"Hmm . . . yes. We are near where we need to be," announced the Wizard.

"How do you know that?" asked The Flash, staring at the strange markings. "They just look like funny pictures to me."

"I know because I drew these . . . *funny pictures*," said the Wizard, sounding annoyed.

The group continued until their path opened into a large circular chamber. The Wizard dropped to his knees and wiped away the sand covering the floor. He revealed a large, six-sided shape.

"This is it!" cheered the Wizard.

"How will this help us?" asked Superman, studying the hexagon.

"This site was once used to summon the ancient gods," answered the Wizard.

"You mean the gods of Egypt?" asked Wonder Woman.

"More than that," replied the Wizard. "Any gods from any culture."

"Do you think it still works?" asked Billy.

"If it does, it should restore my power to take us back home," said the Wizard.

"What do we have to do?" asked Batman.

"The six of you must face the trials of the gods. This will only work if all of you are successful," said the Wizard.

"Great . . . no pressure," said The Flash.

"Hurry. Stand on the six points of the hexagon," said the Wizard. Then he took his place in the middle of the shape.

As each of them stood on their point, the Wizard used a stone to draw a symbol on the floor. At first nothing happened. Then the floor beneath them lit up. In an instant they all disappeared.

* * *

Superman appeared on an island at the base of a towering mountain. Lifting off, he soared past the trees, through the clouds, and up to a stone temple on the summit. A god with white hair and a curly beard awaited him. The god's robe hung off one shoulder, revealing a strong, muscular body.

"Welcome to Mount Olympus and your test," said the god.

"Of course. You're Zeus!" exclaimed Superman.

"We both command great power," said Zeus. "Today we see how powerful you really are. Your test is simple. Remove me from this mountain . . . if you can."

The sky darkened over the temple as Zeus raised a hand to the heavens. A lightning bolt formed between his fingers, and he cast it at Superman. The bolt struck the Man of Steel in the chest, sending him crashing down to the beach below.

KRA·KOOOOOM!

Clutching his smoking chest, Superman struggled back to his feet. He flew back to the summit where thunderbolts rained down on him. He tried punching through the lightning, but it engulfed him in light. He tumbled backward into the ocean below.

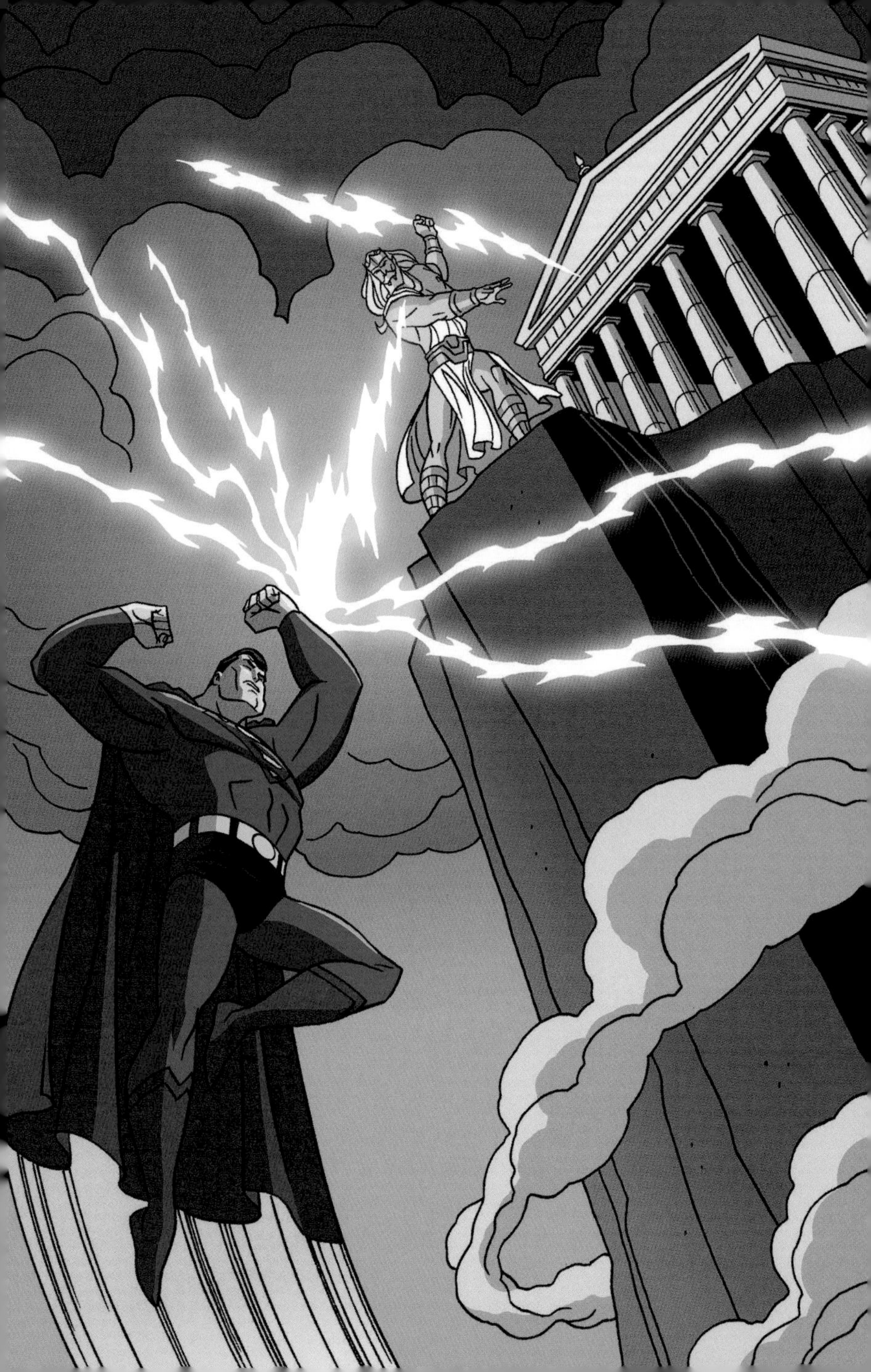

When Superman dragged himself back onto the beach, he was exhausted. He had never felt such raw power. Defeating the father of the gods might be impossible if he couldn't reach him. But maybe he didn't have to.

Superman walked to the base of the mountain. Using his heat vision, he burned a wide swath through the rock. When the stone melted, he gripped the mountain with his hands and shook it with all of his might. As it swayed in his grip, Zeus stumbled and fell from the summit. Superman caught the god in his arms and returned him to the temple.

"You have passed the test," said Zeus. "Let us hope your friends are as successful."

Superman nodded and disappeared.

* * *

Wonder Woman appeared in the halls of a crumbling building. Among the rubble stood a demigod wearing a lion's skin.

"Hello, Hercules," greeted Wonder Woman. "My mother, Hippolyta, would like her belt back."

"Ah yes, the Amazonian queen. Taking her belt was one of twelve labors I completed," boasted Hercules. "What have you accomplished?"

"I've defeated foolish men such as yourself," countered Wonder Woman.

Hercules laughed. "Very well. You will be wrapped in the tightest of chains for your trial. To succeed you must get free. But I don't think you will . . . since I will bind them to you myself. And no one is stronger than the mighty Hercules!"

"Many have tried to tie me down," said Wonder Woman. "All have failed."

It took all of Hercules' strength to wrap a thick metal chain around Wonder Woman. Its weight forced the Amazon warrior's legs to buckle. She fell to her knees.

"This chain once held the three-headed dog, Cerberus, in the underworld," said Hercules. "No one has ever broken free."

Wonder Woman closed her eyes to focus. She struggled to raise one leg and then the other. Finally standing, she flexed her muscles against the chain.

"Hera . . . give me strength!" she shouted.

The links in the chain began to bend, then — **CRACK!** The thick chain snapped off her body, whipping across the room. Hercules ducked as it flew over his head.

"You have passed your trial," said Hercules with a look of disappointment.

"I still want that belt back," said Wonder Woman. Hercules just grinned as she disappeared from the hall.

* * *

Batman appeared in a vast room. Based on the many rows of bookshelves before him, he knew this was a house of learning and knowledge. He turned as a voice welcomed him from behind.

"I am Solomon," said an older man wearing a gold crown and a flowing blue robe. "I have been a king, a prophet, and even a magician. When asked what I desired most, I was gifted the power of wisdom. I now ask you, what is it you desire most?"

Batman remained silent.

"Perhaps it is to be sent home," said Solomon. He waved his hand and a vision of Wayne Manor appeared.

"Perhaps it's to be given power beyond your reach," said Solomon. Now a vision of Batman defeating Black Adam appeared.

"I can even restore those you have loved and lost," offered Solomon. The vision changed to Bruce reuniting with his parents.

"So I ask again . . . what is it you desire?" asked Solomon.

"Justice," Batman answered simply.

Solomon stood quietly, deep in thought.

"You had the chance to get anything for yourself," said Solomon. "Instead, you have chosen something for others. You have passed this trial."

Batman disappeared from the library.

* * *

Green Lantern appeared on a rocky
hilltop bathed in the soft glow of the setting
sun. Standing before him was the mighty
Atlas. The enormous titan had massive
arms and thick legs. All around him stood
boulders of various sizes.

"You know, I once held up the sky for an
eternity," explained Atlas.

"And I once held the chili dog eating
championship of Sector 2814," joked Green
Lantern. "You should be impressed. Some of
those aliens had three stomachs!"

"Enough of your banter," said the titan,
holding a firm upper lip. "For your trial we
shall see who can hold a heavy stone the
longest without dropping it. I must admit,
this trial favors me."

"Says you," said Green Lantern. He used his power ring to create giant, overly muscled arms, which he flexed and posed.

Atlas lifted a giant stone and held it over his head. Green Lantern did the same with the help of his power ring-enhanced arms.

As the sun dipped below the distant horizon, it was clear Atlas could hold his stone forever. But Green Lantern wasn't so lucky. His ring was steadily losing power. And without his lantern nearby, he couldn't recharge it.

Large beads of sweat dripped down the hero's face. He knew he must change his strategy to win this trial.

"Question for you, big guy. Have you ever seen any movies about Greek mythology?" asked Green Lantern.

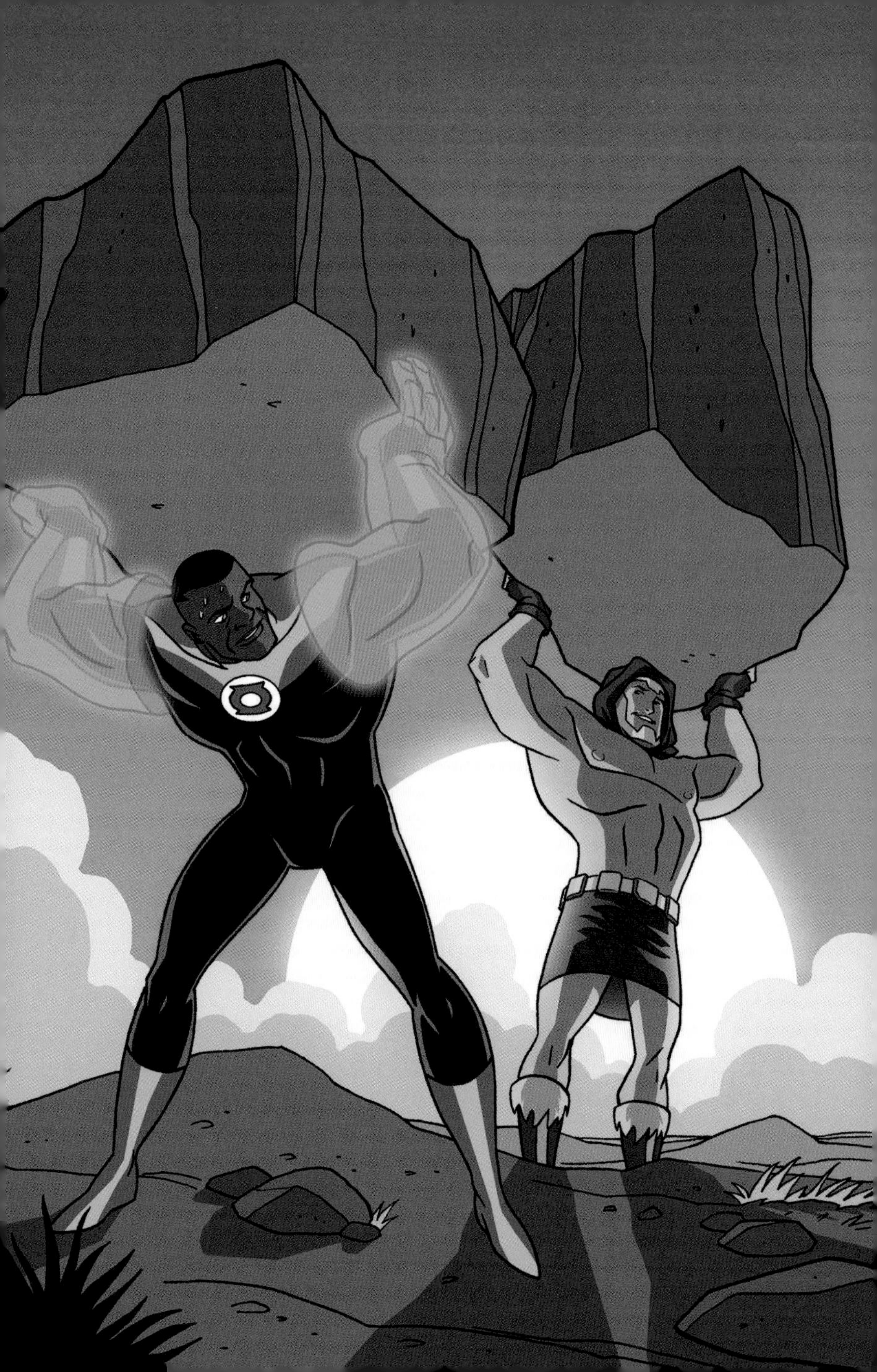

"No," said Atlas very calmly.

"Well that's too bad," replied Green Lantern. "Because I gotta say, you really Odyssey them!"

Atlas smirked as he pondered Green Lantern's response. "Odyssey . . . ," he muttered. Then his lips began to quiver and his grip on the stone slipped slightly.

BWAHAHAH HAAAA!

Atlas dropped his rock and clutched his belly.

"Well played," said Atlas. "You have beaten me at this trial. But please, wound me no more with your jokes."

"You got it," agreed Green Lantern, chuckling to himself as he disappeared.

* * *

The Flash appeared in a vast, dry desert of cracked stone. A god standing nearby beckoned him over. He had wings attached to his helmet and sandals, and he wore a light tunic. They met and shook hands.

"You're Mercury!" exclaimed The Flash. "You're kind of a big thing in the Speed Force . . . the group I'm a part of."

"Care to race?" asked Mercury.

"Anytime, anywhere," said The Flash, puffing out his chest.

"Good," replied Mercury. "Our contest is simple: to see who can circle the globe the fastest." Mercury swiped his foot across the ground. The line marked their starting and ending point.

They both toed the line. Mercury said the countdown, "Three, two, one . . . *GO!*"

Mercury's winged sandals launched him forward. Surprised by his opponent's incredible burst of speed, The Flash instantly fell a half second behind and continued to lose ground.

"Try to keep up," yelled Mercury.

Their bodies blurred into a race between gold and red — and red was trailing. Across oceans, over mountains, and through forests they ran. But The Flash just couldn't gain ground.

At the base of the last mountain range before the finish line, The Flash yelled out to his competitor. "It's been an honor to race you."

"The honor was definitely yours," bragged Mercury. When he heard no reply, Mercury looked over his shoulder. To his surprise, The Flash was gone!

As Mercury came over the top of the mountain, he looked down at the desert. Someone was waving from the finish line.

"I was wondering when you'd show up," said The Flash as Mercury approached. "For a moment there I thought I might have to go out looking for you."

"How did you beat me?" Mercury asked, more stunned than out of breath.

"You never said we had to take the same path," replied The Flash. "I phased through the mountain while you ran over it. My path to the finish line was shorter."

"You passed the trial," said Mercury with a frown. "But I look forward to a rematch."

"You're on!" said The Flash, slapping the god on the back. As Mercury bent down to pick up his helmet, The Flash disappeared.

* * *

Billy appeared on a battlefield of fallen soldiers. Facing him stood a god dressed in heavily plated armor, holding a sword and shield. Leather sandals covered the warrior's feet, and his wide stance showed he was ready to attack.

"What folly is this?" yelled Achilles. "They sent a mortal child to face me?"

Billy swallowed hard. Why did he have to compete when the Justice League heroes were so much stronger? He couldn't defeat this warrior. He might not even live.

"Speak up! With a sword . . . or with your whimpering," challenged Achilles.

You will always lose if you never try, thought Billy. It was something the Wizard always told him when he wavered.

Billy found a sword twice his size on
the battlefield. He struggled to pick it up,
stumbling under its weight. Then he moved
toward Achilles to face him in battle.

CLANGGGG! Achilles knocked Billy's sword
from his hands. Billy fell backward.

"Try again!" yelled Achilles.

Billy crawled along the ground and found
a spear. Maybe he'd stand a better chance
from a distance. Getting a running start, Billy
threw the spear with all his might. It simply
shattered into a dozen pieces when Achilles
blocked it with his shield.

"You cannot defeat me. I am Achilles, a
hero of the Trojan War!" the warrior shouted,
slapping his sword against his shield.

Achilles?! I've read about him at school,
thought Billy. *I might have a chance after all!*

Billy charged at Achilles without a weapon. As the warrior swung his sword, the boy slid under his legs like a baseball player stealing home plate. Now behind the warrior, Billy grabbed a rock and threw it at his enemy's heel.

The rock found its mark. Achilles fell to the ground, dropping his weapon.

"You found my weakness and passed the trial," spat Achilles. "But remember, everyone has a weakness. Not just me."

Billy helped the fallen warrior back to his feet. Then the boy quietly disappeared.

* * *

Inside the pyramid the Justice League and Billy returned to their spots on the hexagon. In the center of the shape, a bright light lifted the Wizard off the ground.

A booming voice echoed throughout the chamber. "S for the wisdom of Solomon. H for the strength of Hercules. A for the stamina of Atlas. Z for the power of Zeus. A for the courage of Achilles. M for the speed of Mercury. All of these have been awarded back to you, Wizard. To claim them . . . say the magic word."

"*SHAZAM!*" shouted the Wizard.

A bright light bathed the room in white, and the Wizard regained his power. He walked over to Billy and placed a hand on his shoulder.

"Thank you, Billy," said the Wizard. "You and your friends have helped restore me. Now let me return the favor to you. Will you be my champion again? If so, just say the magic word."

Billy didn't hesitate. "*SHAZAM!*"

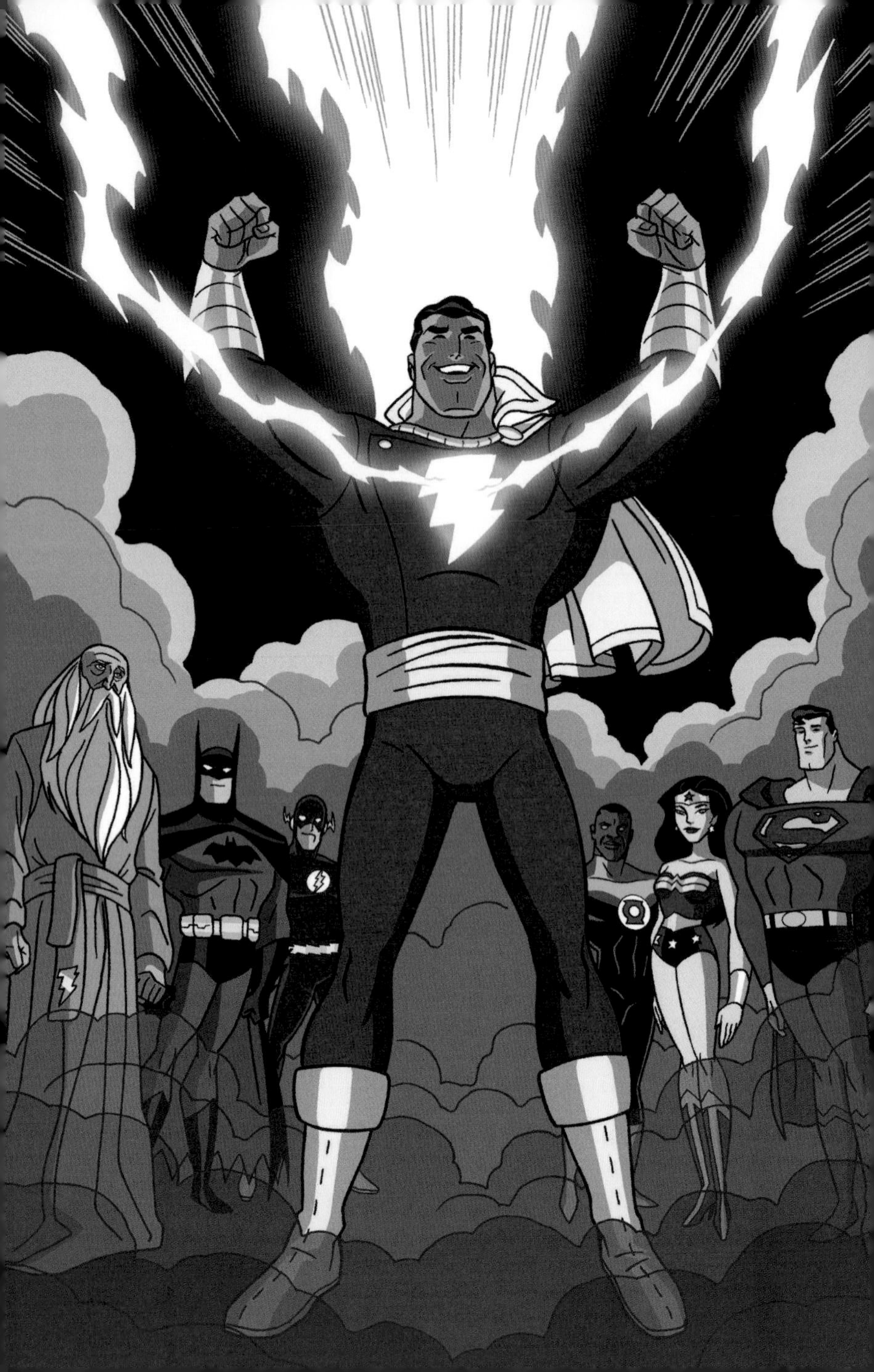

CRACK!

A lightning bolt struck Billy from above. When the smoke cleared, a man dressed in red and gold, with a white cape, emerged. The thunderbolt in the center of his chest marked the return of Earth's Mightiest Mortal . . . the hero Shazam!

The Wizard turned to the Justice League. "Thank you all for doing what needed to be done. Let's go home."

"And stop that rascal, Black Adam," added Shazam with a wink and a smile.

With a snap of his fingers, the Wizard opened a time portal. They all entered it to return home.

CHAPTER 5

BATTLE FOR ETERNITY

"Teth-Adam, get off of my throne!" commanded the Wizard.

The Wizard had returned with the Justice League and Shazam to the Rock of Eternity. Black Adam remained seated, his eyes wide and his eyebrows raised.

"You've found a way back, old man," said Black Adam. "Not that it will do any good."

"Maybe I can help," said Shazam. He flew forward and knocked Black Adam off his seat with a well-placed punch.

"The big red cheese is back as well? Then this will be fun!" exclaimed Black Adam. "But don't worry. I won't leave the rest of you empty-handed."

Black Adam clapped his hands. The stone statues of Pride, Envy, Greed, Hatred, Selfishness, Laziness, and Injustice — the Seven Deadly Enemies of Man — came alive! They climbed off their perch and attacked the Justice League.

Superman raised both fists and flew at Hatred, expecting to explode through the stone statue. Instead, he bounced off of it and fell backward to the floor.

Green Lantern used the last of his ring's power to create a power drill to fend off Selfishness. The statue grabbed the drill, but Envy wanted a piece of the action, too, and tried to tear it away.

The Flash ran circles around Laziness, but the statue used its wide belly to bump the hero out of the way. The speedster crashed into a cave wall.

Wonder Woman battled Pride and Greed. Pride simply folded its arms and smiled as Wonder Woman wrapped her lasso around it. Try as she might she couldn't make the statue budge. Meanwhile, Greed came up behind her and grabbed her in a bear hug.

Batman faced Injustice, an enemy he was all too familiar with. After each stared the other down, they charged one another. They traded blows in a stalemate.

While the Justice League continued to battle the statues, Black Adam grabbed the Wizard and threw him onto the throne.

"Here, have your seat back," the villain said. "And everything that comes with it."

Then Adam blew out the torch next to the throne, making the Wizard disappear. Only with it lit would he return.

"Your friends have met their match. Your Wizard is gone," said Black Adam. "It's just you and me now."

Shazam squinted at his most hated rival. Then he heard the Wizard's friendly voice in his head. *It's up to you to defeat him, Billy. You . . . not Shazam. Find the courage that is within you.*

Shazam dropped his arms. He relaxed his stance.

"SHAZAM!" he said. In a flash of lightning and smoke, the mighty hero transformed back into Billy Batson.

"HA!" laughed Black Adam. "You're just giving up?"

"Never!" Billy said. "Instead, I offer you a trial. If I win, you must leave the Rock of Eternity and never come back. But if I lose, then this world is yours."

"I accept your foolish offer," boasted Black Adam. "What is the challenge?"

"A game," said Billy, carefully drawing a circle on the floor with his foot. "It's called Devin's Doom."

"Who is this *Devin*?" questioned Black Adam. "Never mind. You wish to play a child's game for the fate of the world?"

"Are you afraid?" asked Billy, finding his discarded backpack. He opened the zipper and took out the ball.

"Of course not," scoffed Black Adam. "I am more than prepared to defeat you no matter the game!"

"Then here," said Billy, tossing the ball to Black Adam. "The rules are simple. We each take turns throwing the ball at the other. If you dodge or catch it, you continue. But if the ball hits you or you fall outside the circle, you lose. You go first."

Black Adam clutched the ball in his hand. He smirked as he looked down at his child opponent. Billy stood in the circle, nervously shifting his weight from one foot to the other. If he lost, then everyone would lose. But he remembered Devin's taunt the last time he played this game.

Next time, why don't you try dodging? It's what you're good at.

"Now it's time to meet your doom, Billy. Or should I call you . . . *Devin?*" asked Black Adam. The villain hurled the ball at him with the speed of a god.

Predicting Adam's throw, Billy dropped to one knee. The ball sailed over his head by mere inches, ruffling his hair with the wind it created.

"Beginner's luck," sneered Black Adam.

Billy ignored the villain and picked up the ball. Now it was his turn. The two competitors circled one another, silently gauging each other's next move.

As they circled, Billy kept his eye on the raised rock he'd tripped on earlier. When Black Adam's feet got close to it, Billy stopped and threw the ball wide left. Black Adam dodged right and tripped on the rock. The stunned villain stumbled out of the circle.

"Not fair! You made me lose," shouted Black Adam.

"You did that to yourself," said Billy. "I learn from my mistakes, but you never do."

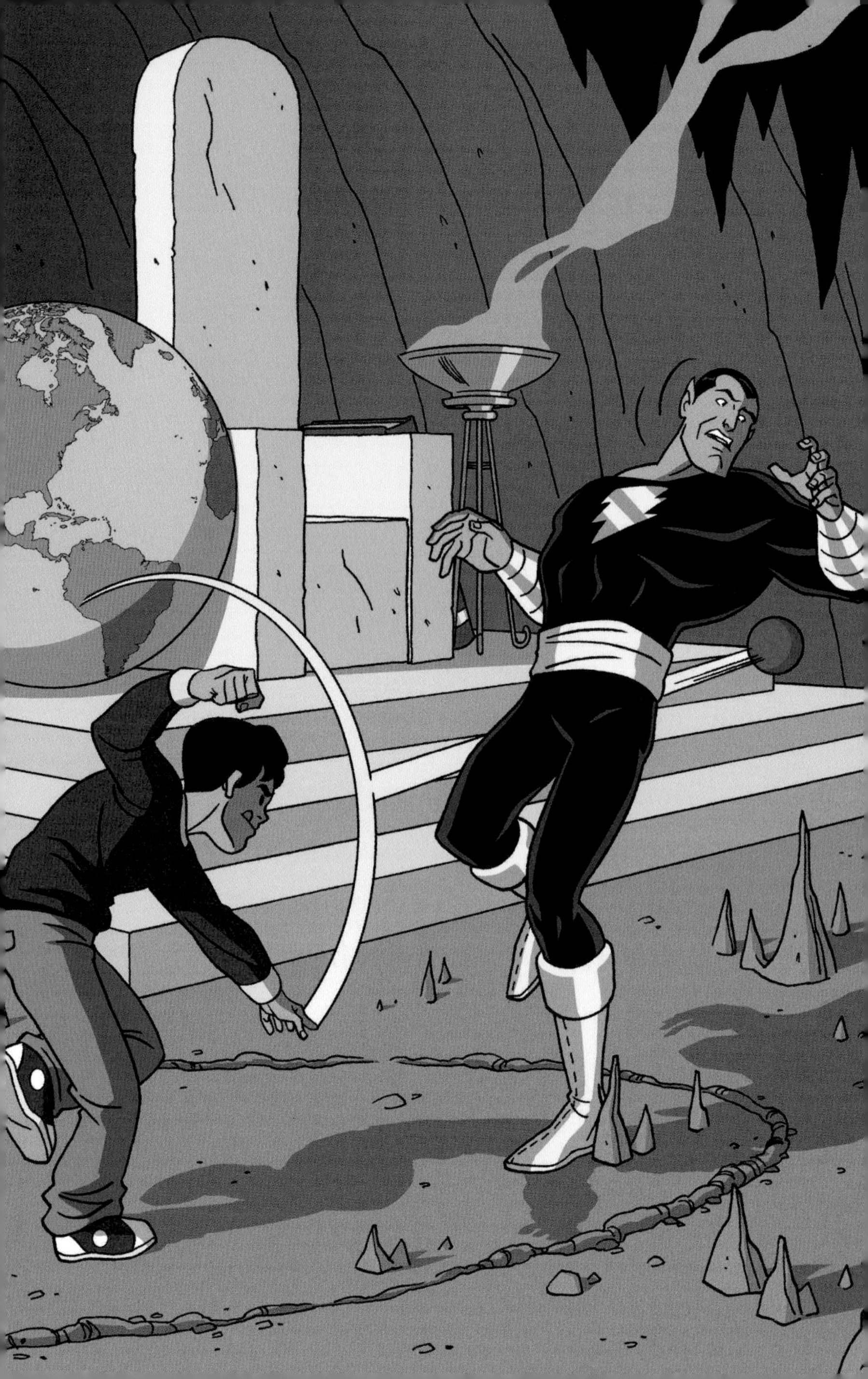

Before Black Adam could back out of their bargain, Billy lit the torch and the Wizard immediately returned. The old man took away Black Adam's power and banished him past the farthest star in space. Then he cast a spell that ended the Justice League's battle by returning the statues to their perch. Finally, he removed all of Black Adam's mummies from the world with a simple spell.

Everything had been restored back to the way it was.

"Thanks for helping us, Billy," said Superman, shaking hands with the boy. "Sometimes we're so used to helping others, we forget that we can use a helping hand ourselves."

"Aw shucks. It was fun," said Billy.

"So, um . . . how do we get out of here?" asked The Flash.

"The train will take you back. And no ticket required," Billy said with a wink.

The Justice League boarded the train and waved goodbye to their friends. Their next stop would be the Watchtower. It took Black Adam five thousand years to return to Earth the last time. They wanted to make sure someone was watching if he made it back sooner next time.

(END)

JL DATABASE: VILLAINS

⟩ **TARGET: APPREHENDED** ⟨

BLACK ADAM

Hailing from ancient Egypt, Teth-Adam was originally chosen by the wizard, Shazam, to become his successor. By saying the magic word "Shazam," Teth-Adam transformed into a being of immense power. But when it was revealed that his evil intent was to rule the world, he was renamed Black Adam. Then the wizard banished him to the farthest star in the universe. In his place a new champion, by the name of Billy Batson, was given the power of Shazam.

LEX LUTHOR   THE JOKER   CHEETAH   SINESTRO   CAPTAIN COLD

BLACK MANTA

AMAZO

GORILLA GRODD

STAR SAPPHIRE

BRAINIAC

DARKSEID

HARLEY QUINN

BIZARRO

THE SHADE

MONGUL

POISON IVY

MR. FREEZE

COPPERHEAD

ULTRA-
HUMANITE

CAPTAIN
BOOMERANG

SOLOMON GRUNDY

BLACK ADAM

DEADSHOT

CIRCE

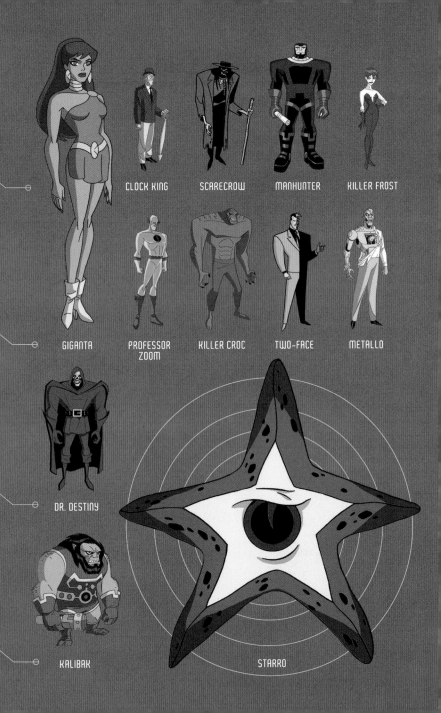

GIGANTA

CLOCK KING

SCARECROW

MANHUNTER

KILLER FROST

PROFESSOR ZOOM

KILLER CROC

TWO-FACE

METALLO

DR. DESTINY

KALIBAK

STARRO

STRENGTH IN NUMBERS

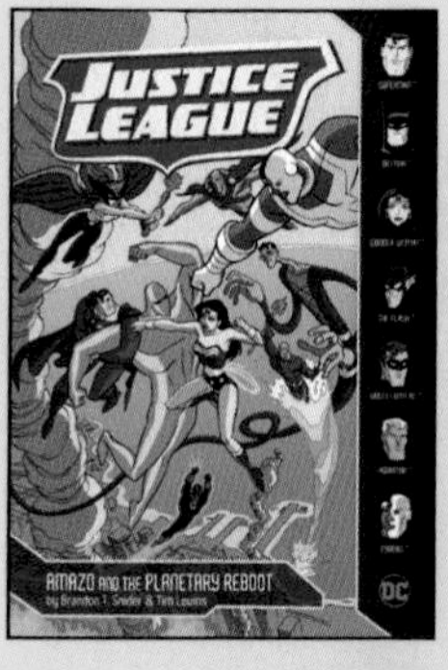
JUSTICE LEAGUE
AMAZO AND THE PLANETARY REBOOT
by Brandon T. Snider & Tim Levins

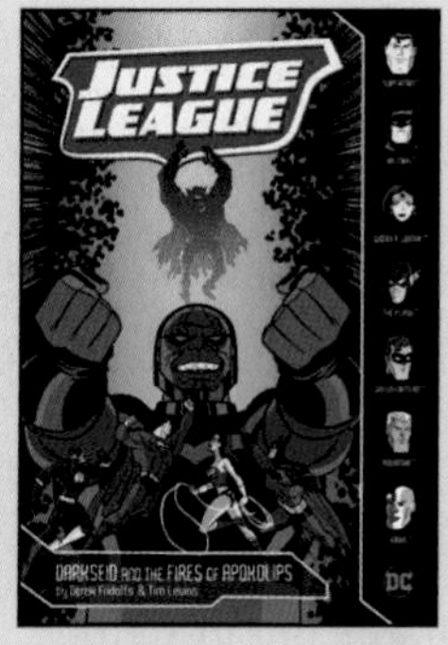
JUSTICE LEAGUE
DARKSEID AND THE FIRES OF APOKOLIPS
by Derek Fridolfs & Tim Levins

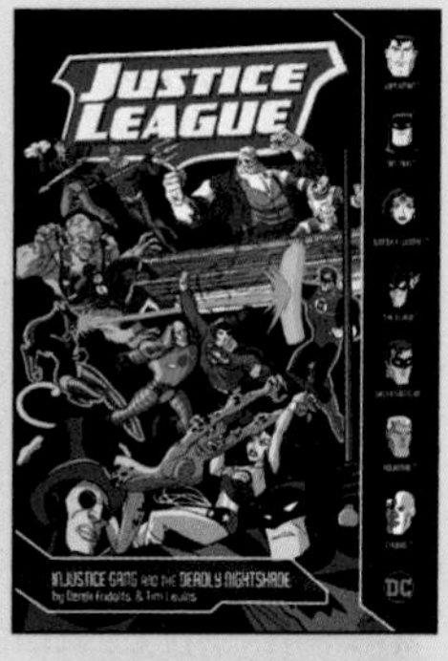
JUSTICE LEAGUE
INJUSTICE GANG AND THE DEADLY NIGHTSHADE
by Derek Fridolfs & Tim Levins

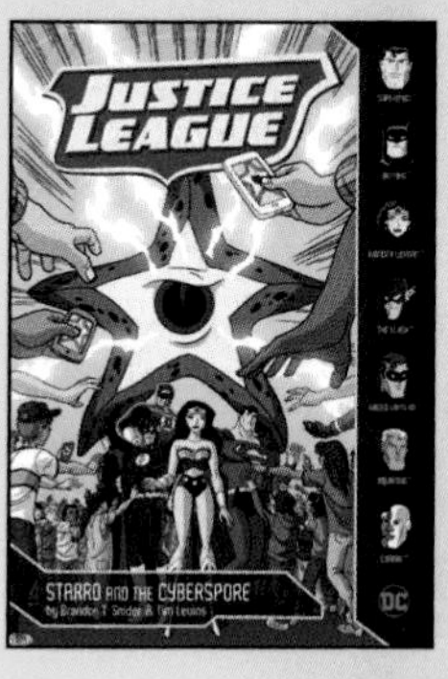
JUSTICE LEAGUE
STARRO AND THE CYBERSPORE
by Brandon T. Snider & Tim Levins

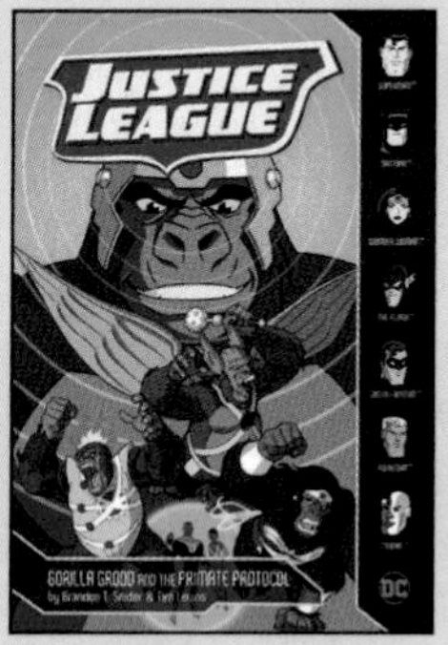
JUSTICE LEAGUE
GORILLA GRODD AND THE PRIMATE PROTOCOL
by Brandon T. Snider & Tim Levins

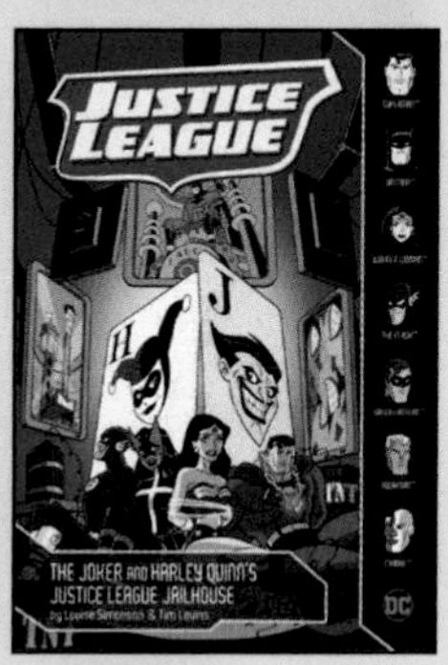
JUSTICE LEAGUE
THE JOKER AND HARLEY QUINN'S
JUSTICE LEAGUE JAILHOUSE
by Louise Simonson & Tim Levins

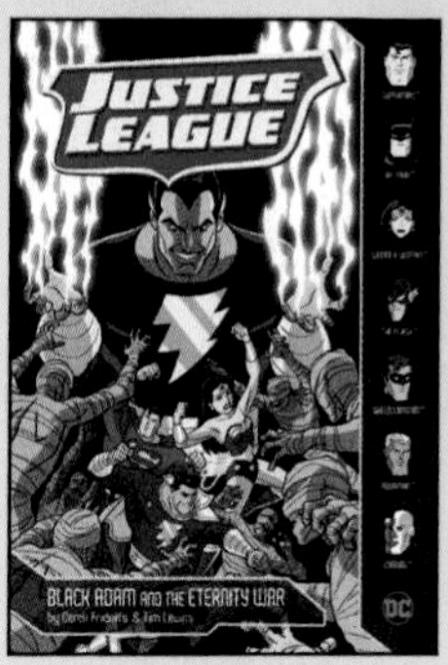
JUSTICE LEAGUE
BLACK ADAM AND THE ETERNITY WAR
by Derek Fridolfs & Tim Levins

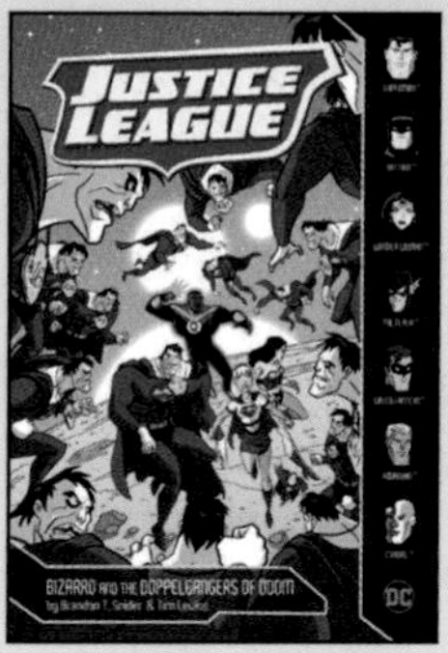
JUSTICE LEAGUE
BIZARRO AND THE DOPPELGANGERS OF DOOM
by Brandon T. Snider & Tim Levins

ONLY FROM capstone

GLOSSARY

banish (BAN-ish)—to send away forever

eternity (i-TUR-nuh-tee)—time without beginning or end

fusion (FYOO-zhuhn)—the joining together of objects caused by heating; the sun creates its energy with the process of fusion

hieroglyph (HYE-ruh-glif)—a picture or symbol used in the ancient Egyptian system of writing

mortal (MOR-tuhl)—human, referring to a being who will eventually die

pharaoh (FAIR-oh)—a king in ancient Egypt

podium (POH-dee-uhm)—a stand used to hold a book or script for someone giving a speech

satellite (SAT-uh-lite)—a spacecraft that circles Earth

sonic (SON-ik)—having to do with sound waves

Sphinx (SFINGKS)—a statue in Giza, Egypt, with the body of a lion and the head of a human

stalactite (stuh-LAK-tite)—a thin piece of rock hanging from the ceiling of a cave

stamina (STAM-uh-nuh)—the energy and strength to keep doing something for a long time

THINK

1. The Justice League uses a variety of ways to defeat the mummies in Metropolis. What other tools and techniques could they have used against them? Discuss which one would have worked best.

2. The Justice League and Billy face off against six Greek gods. Which battle was your favorite? Why did you like it best?

3. Why does Billy use Devin's Doom to challenge Black Adam at the end? What other playground games could he have used?

WRITE

1. If Black Adam sent you back in time, which time period would you want to visit? Write a short story about your adventure.

2. Billy can change into Shazam by saying a magic word. Create your own magic word and write a paragraph describing what you would change into.

3. The Wizard sends Black Adam back to the farthest star in deep space at the end of the story. Write a short story about what the villain does next.

AUTHOR

DEREK FRIDOLFS is the #1 *New York Times* bestselling writer of the DC Secret Hero Society series, and the Eisner nominated co-writer of *Batman Li'l Gotham*. He has worked in comics for more than 15 years as a writer, artist, and inker on such beloved properties as *Adventures of Superman*, *Detective Comics*, *Arkham City Endgame*, *Sensational Comics Featuring Wonder Woman*, *Justice League Beyond*, *Teen Titans Go*, *Scooby-Doo*, *Looney Tunes*, *Teenage Mutant Ninja Turtles*, *Dexter's Laboratory*, *Clarence*, *Regular Show*, and *Adventure Time*. He resides in California's central valley.

ILLUSTRATOR

TIM LEVINS is best known for his work on the Eisner Award-winning DC Comics series Batman: Gotham Adventures. Tim has illustrated other DC titles, such as *Justice League Adventures*, *Batgirl*, *Metal Men*, and *Scooby-Doo*, and has also done work for Marvel Comics and Archie Comics. Tim enjoys life in Midland, Ontario, Canada, with his wife, son, dog, and two horses.